JEASY

De Paola, Tomie.

Andy (that's my name) /

1999.

BY TOMIE DE PAOLA

ANDY
(THAT'S MY NAME)

ALADDIN PAPERBACKS

FOR

D.B.D.

First Aladdin Paperbacks edition August 1999 Copyright © 1973 by Tomie dePaola
Aladdin Paperbacks An imprint of Simon & Schuster Children's Publishing Division
1230 Avenue of the Americas, New York, NY 10020
Printed and bound in the United States of America
10 9 8 7 6 5 4

The Library of Congress has cataloged the hardcover edition as follows:
dePaola, Thomas Anthony. Andy: that's my name.
Summary: Andy's friends construct different words from his name: "an" words, "and" words, and "andy" words.
I. Title. PZ7.D439An [E] 73-4593
ISBN 0-671-66464-6 ISBN 0-689-82697-4 (Aladdin pbk.)

PAN

RAN

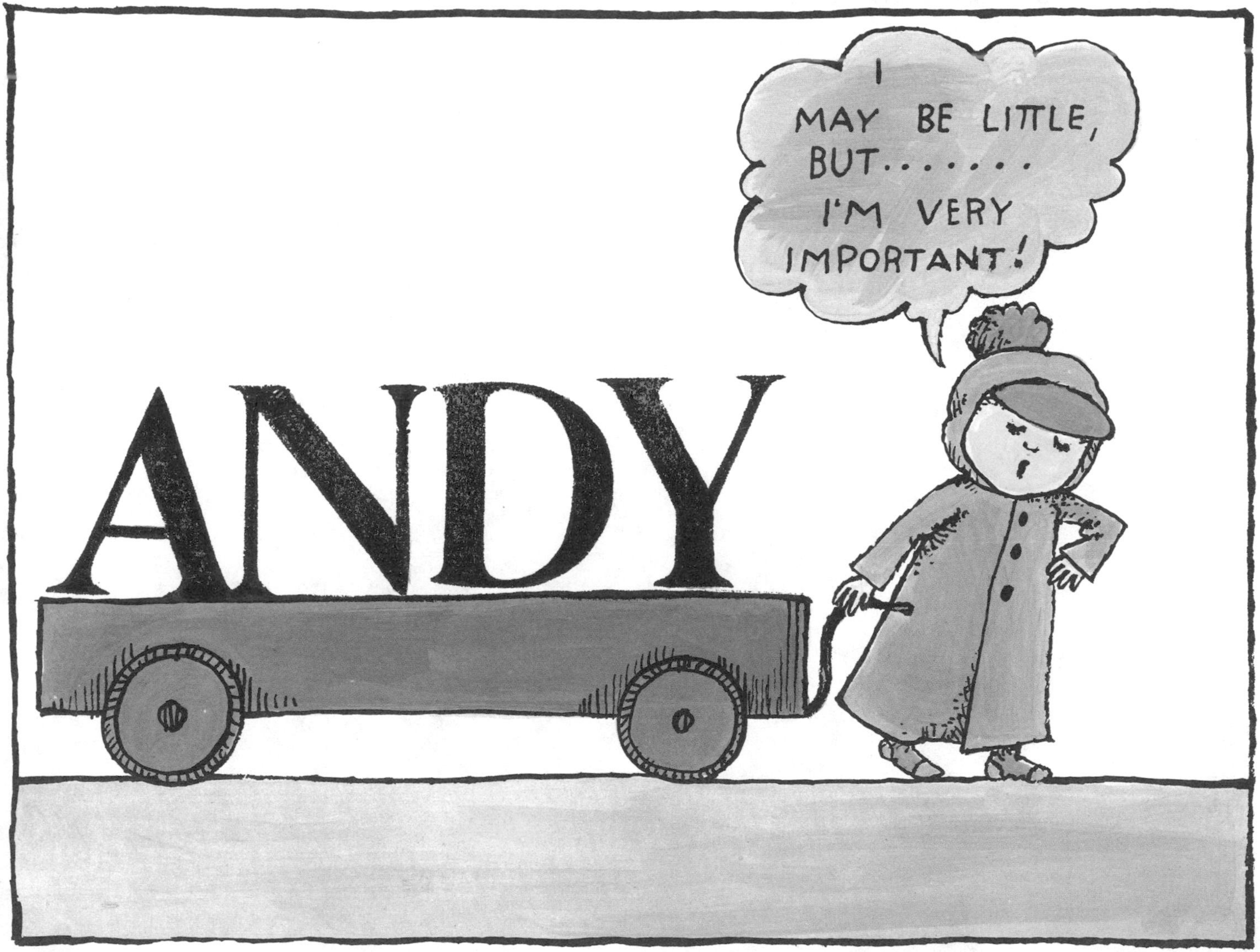
I MAY BE LITTLE, BUT....... I'M VERY IMPORTANT!
ANDY